Dear Reader,

Thank you for choc
Anniversary Edition an
of a cast of everyday people, who, like us, dream, but never know what is going to happen next.

So, Welcome to our 25th anniversary celebration for my Dakota Series.

It is hard to believe twenty-five years have passed since Dakota Dawn hit the mail boxes and bookstores across the country.

But how to celebrate this amazing time? When I have a puzzle, I often ask my reader family and friends for suggestions, this time on how to celebrate. They always come through so here are some of their ideas. Bring the books out again, *but* add something new. Hm-m-m. But what? Some said add more books to the series, someone else suggested new covers. Okay. Giveaways were at the top of some lists. Such great possibilities.

A light bulb went off in my brain. When I am out speaking everyone loves to hear what I call the stories behind the stories. Therefore, this celebration gift to you is the story behind the story. You will find these at the end of each book.

So I wish you happy reading. Thank you for joining me and the folks of Soldahl, North Dakota in 1910.

But that's not the end of the celebration. Watch for news in my email letters, website (laurainesnelling. com), Facebook (Lauraine Snelling, author) and maybe sky-writing and fireworks. Oh, probably not but...

Blessings always,
Lauraine

DAKOTA Destiny

DAKOTA SERIES
BOOK FIVE

DAKOTA
Destiny

LAURAINE
SNELLING

Previously Published in 1993 as Dakota Destiny by Barbour Books, an imprint of Barbour Publishing, 1810 Barbour Drive, Uhrichesville, OH 44683,

Previously Published in 2008 as Dakota Stories II: Dakota Dusk and Dakota December and Dakota Destiny by Smoky Water Press, Bismarck, ND Former ISBN: 978-0-9820752-1-0

Previously Published in 2012 as Dakota Destiny and Dakota December by eChristian, Inc., Escondido, CA 92029 Former ISBN: 978-1-61843-203-2

25th Anniversary Printing in 2018 by Story Architect, 52 Mission Circle, Suite 122, PMB 170, Santa Rosa, CA 95409-5370

ISBN: 9781728727134

Cover Design by: Roseanna White Designs
Interior Design by: Roseanna White Designs

Published in association with the Books & Such Literary Management, 52 Mission Circle, Suite 122, PMB 170, Santa Rosa, CA 95409-5370, www.booksandsuch.com.

Scripture Quotations are from the King James Version of the Bible.

ABOUT THE AUTHOR

Lauraine Snelling is the best-selling author of over seventy books, both fiction and nonfiction, historical and contemporary for adults and young readers. Lauraine and her husband Wayne live in California with a Basset Hound named Annie.

To learn more about the author, you can visit www.laurainesnelling.com. Read all the stories in this series:

Dakota Dawn

Dakota Dream

Dakota Dusk

Dakota December

Dakota Destiny

To today's sons and daughters of the pioneers.

May we always remember those who came before us.

Chapter

ONE

"M ary's home! Mary's home!" Daniel, the youngest of the Moen brood, left off swinging on the gate to the picket fence and leaped up the porch steps to the door. "Mother, did you hear me?"

"Only me and half the town. Must you yell so?" Ingeborg Moen made her way down the steep stairs and bustled over to the door. "Did you see her or was it the little bird that told you?"

"I saw—" A gloved hand clamped gently over his mouth.

"Hello, Mother." Mary stood in the doorway. At seventeen, she had shed the little girl and donned the young woman. Golden hair fell in curls down her back, held back from her oval face with a whalebone clasp, high on the back of her head. Eyes the blue of a Dakota summer sky still shone with the direct look that made students in her Sunday school classes squirm, much as her younger siblings had for years.

There was something about Mary that not only commanded attention but also made one look again. Was it the straightness of her carriage fostered by years of Mrs. Norgaard insisting the girls of Soldahl walk and stand tall no matter what their height? Or the firmness of her chin that bespoke of a will of her own? Or was it the twinkle that hid under long, dark lashes and flirted with the dimple in her right cheek whenever she was trying not to laugh—which was often?

Ingeborg gathered her eldest chick in her arms and hugged her as if they'd been apart for years instead of months. "Oh, my dear, I have missed you so. The house, nay, even the town, is not the same without my Mary." She set the young woman a bit away and studied the girl's eyes. "How have you been, really? Has the school been hard for you? And the train trip home—all went well?"

"Mother, how can I answer so many questions at once? This has been a most marvelous year, and when I finish this time next spring, I will be able to teach school anywhere in North Dakota. Isn't that the most, the most—" Mary threw herself back in her mother's arms. "Oh, much as I love school, I have missed you all sorely."

Daniel thumped her valise on the waxed wooden floor. "Did you bring anything for all of us?"

"Of course I did, and how come you're not in school?" She hugged her ten-year-old brother. "You're not sick, are you? You don't look it."

He pulled away, already at the age of being embarrassed by being hugged in public. "Naw, not much anyway."

Mary looked a question at her mother. This, the baby in the family, had suffered many ailments in his short life. He seemed to catch anything that visited the school or the neighboring children, and with him it always lasted longer and took more of a toll.

"He'll be going back tomorrow." A shadow passed over Ingeborg's placid features. She lived by the creed that God loved His children and would always protect them. She'd taught that belief to her children all their lives, both she and the Reverend John, her husband.

But sometimes in the dead of night when this one of her brood was near death's door, her faith had been tried—and wavered. But such doubts never lingered longer than the rise of the new day, for she believed implicitly in the mansions Jesus had gone to prepare.

Mary sniffed once and then again. "You baked apple pies."

"The last of the barrel. I'd been saving them for you, hoping they would last."

"I helped peel."

Mary stroked Daniel's pale cheek. "And I bet you are the best apple peeler in Soldahl. Now, let me put my things away and we will sample some of Mother's crust cookies, or did you eat them all?"

He shook his head so hard, the white blond hair swung across his forehead. "I didn't."

Mary headed for the stairs. "And you, my dear

Mor, will fill me in on all the happenings of town and country since your last letter."

"Will came by yesterday." Daniel struggled up the steps with the heavy valise.

"He did, eh?" Mary looked up to catch a nod from her mother. A trill of pleasure rippled up Mary's back. *Will, soon I will see Will again. And we will have an entire summer to find out how deep our friendship really goes.*

She turned back to her little brother. "Here, let's do that together. That bag is so burdened with books, no wonder we can't lift it." Mary settled her hand next to Daniel's on the leather grip, and together they lugged it up the steep stairs—Mary laughing and teasing her little brother all the way. They set the case down, and with a sigh of happiness, Mary looked around the room she'd known all her life.

The first nine-patch quilt she'd made with her mother covered the bed, and the rag rug on the floor had warmed her feet since she was ten. Stiffly starched white Priscilla curtains crossed over the south-facing windows, and an oak commode held the same rose-trimmed pitcher and bowl given her by her bestamor, her mother's mother. The ceiling still slanted the same, its rose wallpaper now fading in places.

Daniel stood silently, intuitive as ever of his eldest sister's feelings. When she finished looking around, he grinned up at her. "Didja see anything new?"

Mary looked again. The kerosene lamp still sat on the corner of her dresser. As soon as she unpacked, the brush and hand mirror would go back in place. She looked down at her brother. "What's up, Danny boy?"

He looked at the ceiling directly above her head. She followed his gaze and her mouth fell open. "Electric lights. Far put in the electricity."

"The church board voted."

Since they lived in the parsonage, all improvements

were at the whim and financial possibilities of the Soldahl Lutheran Church. They'd all grown up under that edict.

Mary reached up and pushed the button on the bare bulb hanging from a cord. Light flooded the room. "Now I can read in bed at night." She spun in place, arms outstretched as if to embrace the entire world, or at least her home and family. She swooped Daniel up and hugged him tight. *He is so thin,* she thought. *Has he been worse than mother told me?* He hugged her back and whispered in her ear. "I've missed you so."

"And me you, Bug. Let's go down and have some of that apple pie, if Mor will cut it before dinner." His childhood nickname slipped out; she hadn't called him that in years, but today, today was a time for remembering. Who knew what a magical day like today would bring?

Mary and Daniel, hand in hand, were halfway down

the stairs when the front door opened again and the Reverend John Moen entered, removing his well-used black fedora as he came. Mary put her finger to her lips, and she and Daniel froze in place.

"So, Mother, what's the news? Ummmm, something surely smells good."

As he walked toward the kitchen, Mary and Daniel tiptoed down the stairs.

"Apple pie? For me?"

"Get your fingers out of the crust." The laughter in Ingeborg's voice could be heard by the two creeping nearer.

Mary silently mouthed, *one, two, three,* and she and Daniel burst around the corner. "Surprise!"

"Land sakes alive, look who's here!" John grabbed his chest in mock shock. "Mary, come home at last." He spread his arms and Mary stepped into them, forcing herself to regain some sort of decorum. "Lord love you, girl, but I was beginning to think you were never coming home." He hugged her close and rested his cheek on smooth golden hair. "When did you go and get so grown up?"

Mary blinked against the tears burning the backs of her eyes.

Her father had aged in the months she'd been gone. Deep lines bracketed his mouth, and the few strands of gray at his temples had multiplied. She stepped back, the better to see his dear face. "I'm never too grown up to come home to my family. Even though I've been so busy I hardly have time to turn around, I've missed you all so much."

"Come now, we can visit as we eat. Daniel, John, go wash your hands. Mary, put this in the center of the table, please." Ingeborg handed her daughter a plate of warm rolls, fresh from the oven. Setting a platter with a roast surrounded by potatoes next to her place,

Ingeborg checked to make sure everything was to her liking.

"Mother, you've gone to such trouble. I'll be around here for months." Mary clasped her hand over the back of the chair that had always been hers. "Oh, it feels so good to be home." She counted the places set and looked over at her mother. "Who else is coming?"

"You'll know soon enough." A knock at the door brightened Mor's eyes. "Go answer that while I bring on the coffee."

Mary gave her a puzzled look and went to do as bid.

"Hello, Mary." Will Dunfey's carrot hair had turned to a deep auburn that made his blue eyes even bluer. The smile on his face looked fit to crack the square jaw that he could set with a stubbornness like a bear trap. His shoulders now filled out a blue chambray shirt, open at the neck and with sleeves buttoned at strong wrists.

"Will!" Mary warred with the desire to throw herself into his arms. Instead she stepped back and beckoned him in. He took her hand as he passed, and a shiver went up her arm and straight to her heart. When he took her other hand and turned her to face him, the two shivers met and the delicious collision could be felt clear to her toes.

"So you're finally home." Had his voice deepened in the last months or was her memory faulty?

"Yes." *Say something intelligent, you ninny. This is only Will, you remember him, your best friend?*

"Invite him to the table, Daughter." The gentle prompting came from her mother.

"Oh, I'm sorry." She unlocked her gaze from the deep blue pools of his eyes and, finally coming to herself, gestured him toward the table. "I believe Mother invited you for dinner."

Will winked at her, nearly undoing her again, and

dropping her hands, crossed the room to shake hands with her father. After greeting the Reverend and Mrs. Moen, he took the place next to Mary's as if he'd been there many times.

The thought of that set Mary to wondering. When she started to pull out her chair, Will leaped to his feet to assist her. Mary stared at him. *What in the world?* She seated herself with a murmured "thank you" and a questioning look over her shoulder. Where had Will, the playmate hero, gone, and when had this exciting man taken his place?

Dinner passed in a blur of laughter, good food, and the kind of visiting that said this was not an unusual occurrence. Daniel treated Will much like his bigger brothers, and Ingeborg scolded the young man like one of her own.

Mary caught up on the news of Soldahl as seen through the loving eyes of her father, the slightly acerbic gaze of her mother, and the humorous observations of Will, who saw things from the point of view of the blacksmith and livery, where he worked for Dag Weinlander.

"The doctor was the latest one," Will was saying. "I'm going to have to go to mechanic's school if this drive to buy automobiles continues. You know, at first Dag thought they were a fad, but now that Mrs. Norgaard owns one and expects him to drive her everywhere, he thinks they're the best."

"Mrs. Norgaard bought an automobile?" Mary dropped her fork. "At her age?"

"Now dear, seventy isn't so old when one is in good health." Ingeborg began stacking the dishes.

"She says she has too much to do to get old," John said with a chuckle. "When I think back to how close she was to dying after her husband died...if it hadn't been for Clara, she would have given up for sure."

"That seems so long ago. I remember the classes we had at her house to learn to speak better English. Mrs. Norgaard was determined all the girls would grow up to be proper young ladies, whether we wanted to or not."

"She took me in hand. If it hadn't been for her and Dag, I would have gotten on the next train and kept on heading west." Will smiled in remembrance. "I thought sure once or twice she was going to whack me with that cane of hers."

"Did she really—whack anyone, that is?" Daniel's eyes grew round.

"Not that I know of, but for one so tiny, she sure can put the fear of God into you."

"Ja, and everyone in town has been blessed by her good heart at one time or another." John held up his coffee cup. "Any more, my dear?"

Ingeborg got to her feet. "I'll bring the dessert. You stay right there, Mary."

"Thanks to her that I am at school." Mary got up anyway and took the remainder of the plates into the kitchen.

"And that the church has a new furnace."

"And the school, too," Daniel added.

"Is Mr. Johnston happy here?" Mary had a dream buried deep in her heart of teaching in the Soldahl school, but that could only happen if the current teacher moved elsewhere.

"Very much so. His wife is president of the Ladies' Aid, such a worker." Ingeborg returned with the apple pie. "I'd hate for them to leave. Their going would leave a real hole in the congregation."

Mary nodded. So much for her dream. Surely there would be a school near Soldahl available next year.

They all enjoyed the pie and coffee, with Will taking

the second piece Ingeborg pushed at him. He waved away the third offering.

"Mother, you are the best pie maker in the entire world." Mary licked her fork for the last bit of pie juice. She looked sideways at Will, but he seemed lost in thoughts of his own. Was something wrong?

When she looked at her father at the foot of the table, a look that matched Will's hovered about his eyes. What was going on?

"I better get back to the church. I have a young couple coming by for marriage counseling." John pushed his chair back. "You want to walk with me, Son?"

"Sure." Daniel leaped to his feet.

"I better be getting back to work, too," Will said with a sigh. "Thank you for such a wonderful meal, Mrs. Moen. I will remember these get- togethers for all time."

"Thank you, Will. Mary, why don't you walk Will to

the gate? I'll do the cleaning up here." Ingeborg smiled, but the light didn't quite reach her eyes.

A goose just walked over my grave, Mary thought as she sensed something further amiss.

She locked her fingers behind her back as Will ushered her out the door. An intelligent word wouldn't come to her mind for the life of her.

"So, did you enjoy the last half of school?" Will leaned against the turned post on the porch.

"I loved most every minute of it. I had to study hard, but I knew that." Mary adopted the other post and turned to face him, her back against the warm surface.

Will held his hat in his hands, one finger outlining the brim. When he looked up at her, the sadness that had lurked in the background leaped forward. "Mary, there is so much I wanted to say, have wanted to say for years, and now—" He looked up at the sky as if asking for guidance.

"Will, I know something is wrong. What is it?"

He sat down on the step and gestured for her to do the same. "First of all, I have to know. Do you love me as I love you—with the kind of love between a man and a woman, not the kind between friends and kids?"

Mary clasped her hands around her skirted knees. All the dreaming of this time, and here it was: no preparation, just boom. "Will, I have always loved you." Her voice came softly but surely.

"I mean as more than friends."

"Will Dunfey, understand me." She turned so she faced him. "I love you. I always have, and I always will."

"I had hoped to ask you to marry me." He laid a calloused hand over hers.

"Had hoped?" She could feel a knot tightening in her breast.

"I thought by the time you graduated I would

perhaps own part of the business or one of my own so I could support you."

"Will, you are scaring me." Mary laid her hand over his.

Will looked up at her, his eyes crying for understanding. "I signed up last week."

"Signed up?"

"Enlisted in the U.S. Army to fight against the Germans. They say this is the war to end all wars and they need strong young men." Mary felt a small part of her die at his words.

Chapter
TWO

O h, Will, you can't leave!" The cry escaped before Mary could trap it.

He studied the hat in his hands. "You know I don't want to."

"Then don't." Mary clasped her hands, her fingers winding themselves together as if they had a mind of their own. "I...I just got home."

"I know." He looked up at her, his eyes filled with love and longing. "But they need men like me to stop the Huns. I couldn't say no. You wouldn't really want me to."

Yes, I would. I want you here. I've been looking forward to this summer for months. It made the hard times bearable. But she wouldn't say those words, couldn't say them. No one had ever accused Mary Moen of being selfish. "Of course not." Now she studied her hands. If she looked at him, he would see the lie in her eyes.

A bee buzzed by and landed on the lilac that had yet to open its blossoms.

Will cleared his throat. "I...I want you to know that I love you. I've wanted to tell you that for years, and I promised I would wait until we—" His voice broke. He sighed. "Aw, Mary, this isn't the way I dreamed it at all." He crossed the narrow gap separating them and took her hands in his. "I want to marry you, but that will have to wait until I come back. No, that's not what I wanted to say at all." He dropped her hands and leaned against the post above her. "What I mean is—"

"I don't care what you mean, Will, darling. I will be here waiting for you, so you keep that in your mind. I will write to you every day and mail the letters once a week, if I can wait that long." She grasped the front of his shirt with both hands. "And you will come back to me, Mr. Will Dunfey. You will come back." She lifted her face to his for the kiss she had dreamed of in the many lonely nights away at school.

His lips felt warm and soft and unbearably sweet. She could feel the tears pooling at the back of her throat. *Dear God, please bring him home again. Watch over him for me.*

"We will all be praying for you," she murmured against his mouth. "I love you. Don't you ever forget that."

"I won't." He kissed her again. When he stepped

back, he clasped her shoulders in his strong hands. "I'll see you tonight?"

She nodded. "Come for supper."

She watched him leap off the porch and trot down the walk to the gate. When the gate swung shut, the squeal of it grated on her ears. It sounded like an animal in pain. Maybe it was her.

"Did he say when he was leaving?" Ingeborg asked when Mary finally returned to the kitchen.

Mary shook her head. "And I forgot to ask." She slapped the palms of her hands on the counter. "It's... it's just not fair."

"Much of life isn't."

"But why should our young men go fight a war in Europe?" She raised a hand. "I know, Mother. I read the newspapers, too. Some want us to be at the front and some want us to pretend it's not there. I just never thought we would be affected so soon. Are others of our boys already signed up, too?"

Ingeborg shook her head. "Not that I know of."

"Then why Will?"

"Now that he has, others will follow. He's always been a leader of the young men—you know that."

"But I had such dreams for this summer—and next year..." Her voice dwindled. "And for the years after that."

"No need to give up the dreams." Ingeborg watched her beloved daughter wrestling with forces against which she had no power. "But...but what if..."

The ticking clock sounded loud in the silence. Ashes crumbled in the freshly blacked cast-iron range.

Mary lifted tear-filled eyes and looked directly at her mother. "What if he doesn't come back?"

"Then with God's strength and blessing you will go on with your life, always remembering Will with fondness and pride." Ingeborg crossed to her daughter. "You would not be the only woman in the country with such a burden to bear. Or the world, for that matter. Perhaps if our boys get in and get the job done, there won't be so many women longing for husbands, lovers, and sons."

"How will I do this?" Mary whispered.

"By the grace of God and by keeping busy making life better for others. That is how women always get through the hard parts of life."

Mary looked up at her mother, wondering as always at the quiet wisdom Ingeborg lived. Her mother didn't say things like that lightly. She who so often sat beside the dying in the wee hours of the morning had been there herself when one child was stillborn and another died in infancy. Mary put her arms around her mother's waist and pillowed her cheek on the familiar shoulder. "Oh, Mor, I've missed you more than words could say."

Ingeborg patted her daughter's back. "God always provides, child, remember that."

After supper that night, Mary and Will strolled down the street in the sweet evening air. They'd talked of many things by the time they returned to her front fence, but one question she had not been able to utter. Finally she blurted it out.

"When will you be leaving?"

"Next week, on Monday."

"But this is already Thursday."

"I know."

Mary swallowed all the words that demanded speech. "Oh." Did a heart shatter and fall in pieces, or did it just seem so?

Chapter

THREE

Would her heart never quit bleeding? Mary stood waving long after the train left. Will had hung half out the side to see her as long as he could. The memory of the sun glinting off his hair and him waving his cap would have to last her a good long time. She had managed to send him off with a smile. She'd promised herself the night before that she would do that. No tears, only smiles.

"We are all praying for him," a familiar voice said from behind her.

"Mrs. Norgaard, how good of you to come." Mary wiped her eyes before turning around. She sniffed and forced a smile to her face.

"He's been one of my boys for more years than I care to count," Mrs. Norgaard said with a thump of her cane. "And I'll be right here waiting when he returns, too." A tear slid down the parchment cheek from under the black veil of her hat. With her back as ramrod straight as ever, Mrs. Norgaard refused to give in to the ravages of time, albeit her step had slowed and spectacles now perched on her straight nose.

"Now, then, we can stand here sniveling or we can get to doing something worthwhile. I know you were praying for him as I was, and we will continue to do that on a daily, or hourly if need be, basis. God only knows what's in store for our boy, but we will keep reminding our Father to be on the lookout." She stepped forward and, hooking her cane over her own arm, slid her other into Mary's. "Mrs. Hanson has coffee and some kind of special treat for all of us, so let us not keep her waiting."

And with that the Moens, Dag and Clara, the doctor and his wife, and several others found themselves back at "the mansion," enjoying a repast much as if they'd just come for a party. With everyone asking her about school and life in Fargo, Mary felt her heart lighten. If she'd done what she planned, she'd have been home flat out across her bed, crying till she dried up.

Dr. Harmon came up to her, tucking a last bite of frosted cake into his mouth. Crumbs caught on his mustache, and he brushed them away with a nonchalant finger. "So, missy, what are you planning for the summer?"

"I was planning on picnics with Will, helping my

mother with the canning and garden, and going riding with Will."

Doc nodded his balding head. "That so." He continued to nod. "I 'spect that's changed somewhat." The twinkle in his eye let her know he understood how she felt. "You given thought to anything else?"

Mary looked at him, her head cocked slightly sideways. "All right, let's have it. I've seen that look on your face too many times through the years to think you are just being polite."

"He's never been 'just polite' in his entire life." Gudrun Norgaard said from her chair off to the side. "What is it, Harmon? Is there something going on I don't know about?"

"How could that be? You got your nose into more business than a hive's got bees."

"Be that as it may, what are you up to?" Mrs. Norgaard crossed her age-spotted hands over the carved head of her cane. Dag had made the cane for her the year her husband died, when she hadn't much cared if she'd lived either.

"I think the two of you are cooking something up again." Clara Weinlander, wife of Dag and mother of their three children, stopped beside her benefactress's chair. "I know that look."

Doc attempted an injured air but stopped when he saw the knowing smile lifting the corners of Gudrun's narrow lips. "All right," he said to the older woman. "You know the Oiens?"

"Of course, that new family that moved into the Erickson property. He works for the railroad, I believe. And she has some kind of health problem—ah, that's it." Gudrun nodded as she spoke. "A good idea, Harmon."

Mary looked from one to the other as if a spectator at that new sport she'd seen at school. Even the women played tennis—well, not her, but those who had a superfluous amount of time and money.

Clara came around to Mary and slipped an arm through hers. "Why do I get the feeling they are messing with someone else's life again?"

"It never did you any harm, did it?" Doc rocked back on his heels, glancing over to where Dag, owner of the local livery and blacksmith, now stood talking with the Reverend Moen. Sunlight from the bay window set both their faces in shadow, but that deep laugh could only come from Dag.

"No, that it didn't." Clara agreed. It had taken her a long time to get Dag to laugh so freely. "So, what do you have planned for Mary here?"

"I thought since she didn't have a position for the summer, she might be willing to help the Oiens care for their children. There are two of them: a boy, four, and the girl, two. And perhaps she could do some fetching for the missus. Mrs. Oien resists the idea of needing help, but I know this would be a big load off her mind."

"What is wrong with her?" Mary asked.

"I just wish I knew. She keeps getting weaker, though she has some good days. You think you could help them out?"

"I'll gladly do what I can."

"I figured as much. After all, you are your mother's daughter." Doc Harmon gave her a nod of approbation. "I'll talk with them tomorrow."

That night Mary wrote her first letter to Will, telling him about the party at the mansion and how it looked like she would be very busy that summer after all. As her letter lengthened, she thought of him on the train traveling east. Hoping he was thinking of her as she was him, she went to stand at her window.

"Look up to the Big Dipper every night," he'd said,

"and think of me standing right on that handle, waving to you."

Mary closed her eyes against the tears that blurred the stars above. "Oh, God, keep him safe, please, and thank You." She looked out again, and the heavens seemed brighter, especially the star right at the end of the dipper handle.

Each morning she greeted the day with, "Thank You for the day, Lord, and thank You that You are watching over Will." After that, she was usually too busy to think.

⸻

The Erickson house sported a new coat of white paint, and the yard had not only been trimmed, but the flower beds along the walk were all dug, ready for planting the annuals now that the likelihood of a last frost was past.

I could do that for them, Mary thought as she lingered so as to arrive at the time Doc Harmon had set. *After all, two little children won't take all my time. And Mrs. Norgaard said a woman came to clean and do some of the cooking. I know Clarissa will come help me if I need it.* Clarissa was her younger sister, after Grace. With six children in their family, there was always someone to help out, even with all the work they did around home.

The two cars arrived at nearly the same time. The man getting out of the first wore a black wool coat as if it were still winter. A homburg hat covered hair the color of oak bark and shaded dark eyes that seemed to have lost all their life. His smile barely touched his mouth, let alone his eyes. Tall and lean, he stooped some, as if the load he bore was getting far too heavy.

Dr. Harmon crossed the grass to take Mary's arm and guide her to meet her host. "Kenneth Oien, I want you to meet Mary Moen, the young woman who has agreed to help you for the summer." As the introductions were completed, Mary studied the man from under her eyelashes. Always one to bring home the stray and injured—both animals and people—Mary recognized pain when she saw it.

"Thank you for coming on such short notice. As the doctor might have told you, my wife, Elizabeth, has not wanted to have help with the children. I finally prevailed upon her to let me hire a woman to clean and do some of the cooking. I'm hoping you can make her days a bit easier. She frets so."

"I hope so, too."

"I...I haven't told her you were coming."

Mary shot a questioning look at the doctor, who just happened to be studying the leaves in the tree above. *I thought this was all set up. What if she hates me?*

"Perhaps you could just meet her and visit awhile, then come back tomorrow after I see how she responds?"

"Of course," Mary answered, still trying to catch the good doctor's attention.

"I'd best be going then—got a woman about to deliver out west aways." Doc tipped his hat. "Nice seeing you, Kenneth, Mary." He scooted off to his automobile before Mary could get in a word edgewise.

Mr. Oien ushered Mary into the front room of the two-story square home. "Elizabeth, I brought you company."

"Back here," the call came from a room that faced north and in most houses like this one was a bedroom. A child's giggle broke the stillness, followed by another.

When they entered the room, the little ones were playing on a bench at the foot of the bed where Elizabeth lay.

"I'm sorry, Kenneth, I was so weak, I had to come back to bed before I fell over."

"Did you eat something?"

She shook her head.

"Have the children eaten?"

"We ate, Papa." The little boy lifted his head from playing with the Sears catalog.

The little girl scooted around the bed and peeped over the far side.

"Elizabeth, Jenny, and Joey, I brought you some company. This is Mary Moen, just returned from college where she is studying to be a teacher."

Elizabeth smoothed her hair back with a white hand. "I...I wasn't expecting company. Please forgive me for... for—" She made a general gesture at her dishevelment and the toys spread about the room.

"I'm sorry, but I have to get back to my job. There is no one else there, you see, and I—" Mr. Oien dropped a kiss on his wife's forehead, waved to the children, and vanished out the door.

Mary heard the front door close behind him. So much for that source of help. She looked around for a chair to draw up to the bed. None. The little girl, Jenny, peered at her from across the bed, nose buried in the covers so all Mary could see was round brown eyes and uncombed, curly hair.

"Jenny don't like strangers," Joey announced from his place on the bench.

"I'm sorry, Miss Moen, I—" Elizabeth sighed. "I know Kenneth is trying to help, but he so often doesn't know how." She shook her head. "But then who would?"

"Sometimes talking to another woman helps." Mary came closer to the bed. "Doctor said you have a woman who comes in to clean."

"She is nice enough, a good worker, but she speaks Norwegian, and I don't. My grandmother came from Sweden and Kenneth's grandparents from Norway. He only knows the table grace and a few phrases. Dear God, I don't know what we are going to do."

Mary nodded. "Well, I know what I am going to do. I didn't come here just to visit. I came to help, and you and I will do much better if we are honest up front. Dr. Harmon and Mrs. Norgaard have a habit of fixing things in people's lives, and they decided I could help you and that way I would be too busy this summer to miss my Will, who left on the train three days ago to fight the Germans."

She felt a thrill at saying the words *my Will* out loud. In the secret places of her heart, he'd been her Will since she was ten and he stuck up for her the first time. She looked around the room again. "How about if I move a chair in here for you to sit in while I fix your hair? Then you can hold Jenny while I brush hers."

"I combed my own hair." Still Joey didn't look up. Though he just kept turning the pages of the catalog, he was obviously keeping track of the conversation.

"Are you sure you want to do this?" Elizabeth asked, the ray of hope peeping from her eyes belying the words.

"Ja, I am sure."

By noon when Kenneth came home for dinner, his wife had a smile on her face, Jenny wore a ribbon in her hair, and Joey had helped set the table. Mary took the chicken and dumplings from the stove and set the pot in the middle of the table.

"My land, why I...I..." He clasped his wife's hand and sat down beside her at the table.

"Thank you, Kenneth. You brought us a miracle worker."

"Mary said—" Joey slid into his place.

"Miss Moen," his father corrected him.

"Oh." A frown creased his forehead. "She said her name was Mary."

Mary set a platter of sliced bread next to the stew pot. "Okay, we can all say grace and then eat. How's that?" She took the chair closest to the food, just as her mother had always done, so she could serve.

"Mary, you are indeed an answer to prayer," Elizabeth said, extending her hand when Mary was ready to leave for home.

"You want me to come back then?"

"With all my heart."

Mary thought about the Oien family as she walked home in the late afternoon. Mr. Larson, the banker, tipped his hat as he passed her on the way home. Mrs. Johnson called hello from the door of the general store, and Miss Mabel waved from behind her display of hats in the ladies' Shoppe. How good it felt to be home, where she knew everyone and everyone knew her.

That night around the supper table, Knute, the oldest of the Moen boys, announced, "I want to enlist like Will did, before there ain't no more Germans to fight."

Mary's heart sprung a new crack. Not her brother, too.

Chapter

FOUR

Y ou have a letter!" Daniel met her halfway home a few evenings later. "From Will?" Mary broke into a run to meet him. A raised eyebrow from the hotel manager made her drop back to a decorous walk.

Daniel skidded to a stop, his cheeks pink from the exertion. "It is, it is! Read it aloud."

"How about if I read it first to myself and then to you?"

"Awww, Mary. I want to know how he is. Does he like being a shoulder?"

"Soldier, Danny boy, soldier." Mary grinned down at him. She slit the envelope with care and pulled out a flimsy sheet of paper. Well, Will certainly wasn't one to waste words on paper any more than he did in person. Working with Dag Weinlander had taught him many things through the years, including how to conserve energy and speech.

My dearest Mary. The word dearest sent a thrill clear to the toes of her black pointed shoes.

> *I cannot not tell you how much I miss the sight of your sweet face. When you were away at school, I always knew that if I grew desperate enough, I could take a train to Fargo and see you, if only briefly. Now I am clear across the continent from you, and so I commend you to the care of*

our loving God, for He can be with you when I cannot.

Mary dug in her bag for a handkerchief.

"Is Will sick? Something is wrong." Daniel backpedaled in front of her so he could watch her face.

"No, silly, it's just that I miss him."

"Oh." He turned and walked beside her, slipping his hand in hers in spite of being out in public.

Mary continued reading.

I never dreamed people could be so ferocious with each other. The sergeants here shout all the time and expect us to do the same. When I think we are being trained to kill our fellowmen, my soul cries out to God to stop this war before anyone else dies. But the Huns must be stopped or the world will never be a safe place in which to love and raise our children.

Mary tucked the letter in her pocket. She would have to finish reading it later when she could cry along with the heartfelt agony of the man she loved. Will had never been afraid to stand up for the weaker children, and he was carrying that same strength into the battle for freedom.

That night she could not see the Big Dipper; clouds covered the sky.

Within a week Mary had both Joey and Jenny waiting by the front windows for her arrival. Mrs. Oien brightened when her young friend walked into the room, and she seemed to be getting stronger. While she sometimes slipped into staring out the window, she more often read to the children and would pinch her cheeks to bring some color to them before Mr. Oien returned home for dinner.

"How would it be if I took the children home to play with my brothers and sisters this afternoon?" Mary asked after dinner one day. "We have a big swing in our backyard, and the cat in the stable has new kittens."

"Kittens." Joey looked from his father to his mother, his heart in his eyes.

"Now, no pets. Your mother has plenty to do already." Mr. Oien effectively doused the light in the child's eyes.

"You can play with them at my house; they are too little to leave their mother yet." Mary stepped into the breach. As far as she was concerned, an animal might make things more lively in this often-silent home. Her mother had never minded when the children brought home another stray—of any kind. In fact, she frequently brought them home herself.

"Perhaps you would like to come, too," she said to Elizabeth. "I know you would love visiting with my mother."

"Another time, dear, when I am feeling stronger."

Elizabeth smiled at her children. "But you two go on and have a good time."

Walking down the street with a child's hand in each of hers, Mary pointed out the store, the post office, and the hotel. But when she passed the livery, all she could think was that Will wasn't the one pounding on the anvil out back, most likely fitting shoes to one of the farmer's horses.

Jenny refused to leave the kittens. She plunked her sturdy little body down by the nest the cat had made in the hay under the horse's manger and giggled when the kittens nursed. She reached out a fat little finger and stroked down the wriggling kittens' backs.

Ingeborg had come out to the stable with Mary to watch. "I can't believe one so little would have the patience to sit like that. She is just enthralled with the kittens."

Joey had looked them over and then gone to see

what the boys were doing. Knute was hoeing weeds in the garden and Daniel followed behind on hands and knees, pulling out the weeds too close to the plants for the hoe to work. He showed Joey which were weeds, and the little boy had followed the older one from then on. When they found a worm, Joey cupped it in his hands and brought it to Mary.

"Did you ever see such a big worm?" he asked.

"I think tomorrow we will dig in your flower beds and perhaps find some there." Mary stroked the hair back from the boy's sweaty forehead. Pulling weeds in the June sun could be a hot task.

"Not this big. This is the biggest worm ever. Can I take it home to show Mama?"

Mary nodded. But when Joey stuck the wriggling worm in his pocket, she shook her head. "He'll die there. Come on, let's find a can for him, and you can put dirt in it." By the time Ingeborg called the children in for lemonade, Joey had several more worms in his can.

"Mor, could we take Joey fishing?" Daniel asked, wiping cookie crumbs from his mouth. All had gathered on the porch for the afternoon treat.

Ingeborg looked up. "I don't see why not. Mary, where is Jenny?"

Mary put her finger to her lips and pointed to the barn. When she and her mother tiptoed into the horse stall, they saw Jenny on the hay, sound asleep. The mother cat and kittens were doing the same.

"I checked on her a few minutes ago and decided to leave her there. Isn't she a darling?"

"You children used to love to sleep in the hay, too. How is their mother, really?"

Mary shook her head. "She scares me sometimes, Mor. It's as though she isn't even there, and other times she is so sad. I don't know what to do to help her." Mary pondered the same question that night when she added to the week's letter to Will. "I wonder about Elizabeth Oien," she wrote. "She loves her husband and children but seems to be slipping away from them. What makes one person have such a strong will to live, like Mrs. Norgaard, and another unable to overcome a bodily weakness? Doc says she has never been the same since Jenny was born. I guess it was a hard time and she nearly died. But the children had such fun at our house."

She went on to describe the afternoon. She closed the letter as always, "May God hold you in His love and care, Your Mary."

Joey caught two fish and a bad case of hero worship. Jenny pleaded every day, "Kittens, pease, see kittens." Daniel spent as much time at the Oiens as he did at home. And Mr. Oien paid Mary double what they'd agreed.

"I cannot begin to tell you what a difference you have made in our lives," he said one evening when he handed her the pay envelope. "Elizabeth and I are eternally grateful."

The Fourth of July dawned with a glorious sunrise, and the rest of the day did its best to keep up. The parade started in the schoolyard and followed Main Street to the park, where a bandstand had been set up. There would be speeches and singing, races for the children, carnival booths set up to earn money for various town groups like the Lutheran church ladies, who sold fancy sandwiches and good strong coffee. Mary had worked in that booth since she was old enough to count the change.

The Grange sold hot dogs, the school board ice cream that was being hand-cranked out behind the booth by members of the board, and the Presbyterian church made the best pies anywhere. Knute won the pie-eating contest for the second year in a row, and one child got stung by a bee. The fireworks that night capped a day that made Mary dream of Will even more. Last year they'd sat together, hands nearly touching while the fireworks burst in the sky to the accompaniment of the band. Did they have fireworks in the training camp he was in?

The next day an entire train car of young men left, waving to their families and sweethearts. They were on their way to an army training camp.

Mary stood next to her father, who had given the benediction at the ceremony. "Soon we won't have any young men left," she said softly. "Who is going to run the farms and provide food for the troops if all the workers leave?"

"Those of us left at home. It is the least we can do." John Moen blew his nose. "God have mercy on those boys." He used his handkerchief to wipe the sweat from his forehead. "Unseasonably hot, isn't it?"

"Yes, Father, it is hot, but you can't fool me. That wasn't all sweat you wiped from your face."

"You are much too observant, my dear. You will make a fine teacher; the children will accuse you of having eyes in the back of your head." John took his daughter's arm on one side and his wife's on the other. "Let's go home and make ice cream. I only got a taste yesterday."

The heat continued, made worse by air so full of moisture it felt like they were breathing underwater. Heat lightning danced and stabbed, but it failed to deliver the needed rain. How hot it was became the talk of the town. When the farmers came in to shop on Saturdays, their horses looked as bone-weary as the people.

Mary tried to entertain the Oien children, but Jenny

fussed and pleaded to go see the kittens. Mrs. Oien lay on the chaise lounge on the back porch, where it was coolest, but daily Mary watched the woman weaken.

If only it would rain. Dust from the streets coated everything, including the marigolds and petunias she had planted along the front walk. Early each day she carried water to the struggling plants, praying for rain like everyone else.

The cornfields to the south of town withered in the heat. Storm clouds formed on the western horizon but always passed without sending their life-giving moisture to the ground below.

One day Mary came home from the Oiens to find Daniel lying in bed, a wet cloth on his forehead. He looked up at her from fever-glazed eyes. "I don't feel so good, Mary."

The letter lying on the hall table had no better news.

Will was boarding the ship to Europe in two days. She checked the postmark. He was already on the high seas.

FIVE

He's a mighty sick boy, Ingeborg, I won't deny that."
Doc Harmon looked up after listening with his
stethoscope to Daniel's labored breathing. "People seem
to fall into a couple of characteristics. Everything seems
to settle in the chest for some, in the stomach for others.
I don't understand it, but with Daniel here, it's always
the chest. Onion plaster might help; keep his fever down
and thump on his chest and back like this to loosen the

mucous." He cupped his hand and tapped it palm down on the boy's back.

Daniel started to cough after only a couple of whacks, giving the doctor a look of total disbelief.

"I know, son, but you will breathe better this way. Make sure he drinks a lot of water, and keep him as cool as possible. That plaster will heat him up some." He looked Daniel in the eye. "Now you do as your mother says and make sure you eat. Lots of broth—both chicken and beef—are good for building him back up."

He looked back up at Ingeborg. "You take care of yourself, too. This summer complaint is affecting lots of people. What we need is a good rain to clear the air."

The rains held off.

Daniel was finally up and around again but more than willing to take afternoon naps. His favorite place was next to Mary. Mrs. Oien seemed better, too, at least in the early morning and after the sun went down. Mr. Oien bought a newfangled gadget called an electric fan.

Everyone wanted to sit in front of it, even when it only moved hot air around. Mary set a pan of water in front of the fan, and that helped them cool more.

July passed with people carrying water to their most precious plants and the farmers facing a year of no crops. At the parsonage, that meant there was no money in the church budget to pay the pastor, and Mary's wages became the lifeline for the Moens.

The weather changed when walnut-sized hailstones pounded the earth and all upon it. What the drought hadn't shriveled, the hail leveled. Ingeborg and Mary stood at the kitchen window and watched the garden they'd so faithfully watered be turned to flat mud and pulp.

"Guess we take God at His word and trust that He will provide." Ingeborg wiped a tear from her eye and squared her shoulders. "The root crops will still be good, and we already had some beans put up. I lived without tomatoes for years, so I know we can do so again. And the corn, well, next year we'll have corn again. At least the early apples were plentiful and perhaps we can buy a barrel from Wisconsin or somewhere later in the fall."

Mary knew her mother was indulging in wishful thinking. There would be no money for apples this year. "Mor, I could stay home from school and keep working for the Oiens."

Ingeborg shook her head. "No, my dear, your school is paid for, and you must finish. If it comes to that, I could go take care of her and those little ones."

Her face lost the strained look of moments before. "See, I said the Lord provides. What a good idea. All of ours are in school all day. Why I could do all their cleaning and cooking and perhaps—no, I couldn't cause someone else to lose their job. We will make do."

Mary knew this talking to herself was her mother's way of working things out, whether anyone else listened or not. She often found herself doing the same thing. Each night when she wrote her letters to Will, she sometimes spoke the words as she wrote them, as if that made him hear them sooner. Or rather see them.

It rained for two days, much of the water running off because the earth was too hard to receive it. At night she stood in front of her window and let the cool breeze blow over her skin. Cool, wet air—what a blessing. But she had to remember where the handle to the Big Dipper lay because she couldn't see it through the clouds.

Why hadn't she heard from Will? Where was he?

She still hadn't heard from him when she packed her trunk for the return to school. She wrapped the three precious letters carefully in a linen handkerchief and tied them with a faded hair ribbon. While she'd about memorized the words, she'd reread the pages until the folds were cracking from repeated bending.

Each week she mailed another letter to him, in care of the U.S. Army. Was he getting her letters? They hadn't come back.

The night before she was to leave, she walked to the mansion" and up to the front door. Fireflies pirouetted to the cadence of the crickets. Mosquitoes whined at her ear, but she brushed them away. She barely raised her hand to knock when Dag swung open the door.

"Come in, come in. Gudrun has been waiting for you." He turned to answer over his shoulder. "Yes, it is Mary." When he ushered her in, he whispered. "I told you she'd been waiting."

"Sorry, I should have come sooner."

"She's in the library."

Mary nodded. She loved coming to this house with its rich velvets and artfully carved sofas and whatnot tables. The embossed wallpaper gleamed in the newly installed electric lights that took the place of the gas jets.

Mrs. Norgaard sat behind the walnut desk that had belonged to her husband when he owned the bank. While she still shared ownership of the Soldahl Bank, her partner managed it and only reported to her once a week, unless of course, there was an emergency.

"Come in, my dear and sit down." She took off her spectacles and rubbed the bridge of her nose. "I'm glad you could humor an old woman like me this last night you have with your family."

"They will see me off in the morning." Mary took in a deep breath and voiced something that had been on her heart and mind for the last weeks. "If paying my school expenses is a hardship for you this year, I could stay—"

"Absolutely not. You will finish your year out, and

then you can teach. The children of North Dakota need teachers like you. If you think a few months of drought and then a hailstorm will wipe out commerce around here, you just don't understand the world yet.

"Companies make a great deal of money during wartime—I sometimes think that is why men start them—and our bank has invested wisely. I can afford your schooling, and you will not hear of my bank foreclosing on the farmers because they can't make their payments on time this year. Or anyone else for that matter. I hear your mother is going to take over at the Oiens?"

Mary nodded.

"That is good. But I have a feeling you've been worrying about the church paying your father's salary." She tipped her head to look over the tops of her gold wire spectacles.

"Some. My mother says they will make do, but I

know it is hard to feed seven mouths, and five of the children are growing so fast we can't keep them in shoes."

"You are not to worry. If I'd known John hadn't gotten paid last month, it never would have happened, and you can bet your life it won't happen again." Mrs. Norgaard sat up straighter. "Those men can bungle things up so bad sometimes, it takes me weeks to just figure it out."

Mary knew she referred to the deacons who ran the business of the congregation. "How'd you find out?" Curious, Mary leaned forward in her chair.

"I have my ways, child."

"Doc Harmon?" Mary shook her head. "No, he's not on the board. Mr. Sommerstrum?" At the twinkle in Gudrun's eye, Mary laughed. "Mrs. Sommerstrum."

"I'll never tell, but it's a good thing some men talk

things over with their wives, even if it's only to share the gossip."

Mary nodded. "I see. I've often wondered how you keep such good tabs on the goings on in Soldahl when you don't go out too often. Mrs. Sommerstrum tells Mrs. Hanson, and Mrs. Hanson tells you." Mrs. Hanson had been the housekeeper at the mansion ever since Mary could remember.

Gudrun nodded. She reached in a drawer, removed an envelope, and handed it across the shiny surface of the desk. "Here. And I don't want you scrimping and going without to send part of that money home, you understand me?"

Mary nodded, guilt sending a flush up her neck. *How did she know what I'd been thinking of?*

"Ah, caught you, did I?" At the girl's slight nod, Gudrun continued. "Now that we have that out of the way, I have a very personal question to ask. Have you heard from Will?"

"No, not since early July, and that letter had been written while he was on the ship."

"Neither have we. That's not like our Will." She stared at the desk before her. "Did he say anything about where they were sending him?"

Again, Mary shook her head.

Gudrun nodded and rose to her feet. "Well, as the old saying goes, no news is good news. Come, let's have a last cup of coffee and some of Mrs. Hanson's angel food cake. I think she has a packet ready to send with you, too."

By the time Mary said good-bye to the family in the mansion, she could hardly hold back the tears. It wasn't like she was going clear around the world or anything, but right now Fargo seemed years away.

The next morning was even worse. Daniel clung to

her until they were both in tears. John finally took the child in his arms while Ingeborg hugged her daughter one last time. Mary smiled through her tears and ruffled Daniel's hair while at the same time hugging her father. She went down the line, hugging each of her brothers and sisters. "Now, promise me, all of you, that when I ask your teacher at Christmas time how you are doing, he will have a good report for me."

They all nodded and smiled at her.

"Hey, I'm not leaving forever, you know."

"It just seems like it."

The train blew its whistle, and the conductor announced, "All aboard."

Mary stepped on the stool and up the stairs. She waved one last time and hurried inside so she could wave again out the window. Slowly the train pulled out of the station, and when she could see them no more, she sank back in her seat to wipe her eyes. Why was leaving so hard when she had so much to look forward to?

As the miles passed, she thought back to the last night she had seen Will. The small package she'd given him contained one of her treasures, the New Testament given her by her parents on her twelfth birthday. "Will you keep this with you to remind you always how much I love you and how much more God loves you?"

"I will keep it in my shirt pocket," he'd replied, never taking his gaze from hers while he put the Testament next to his heart. "But I need no reminder."

The kiss they'd shared had been only sweeter with the small book tucked between them.

At Grand Forks, two of Mary's friends from the year before boarded, and they spent the remainder of the trip catching up on their summers. When Mary told them Will had gone to war, Janice said her brother had left, too. Dorie shook her head. "I can't believe all our boys are going over there. What if they don't come home? Who will we marry?"

Mary rolled her eyes. "Leave it to you to keep the most important things right out front." The three laughed, but Mary felt a pang of fear. What if Will didn't come home?

One evening, toward the middle of October, she returned to her room to find a message saying there was a gentleman waiting in the parlor. He wanted to talk with her. Mary flew back down the stairs, her heart pounding. Perhaps it was Will!

But when she slid open the heavy door, her father and Dag Weinlander sat in the armchairs facing the fireplace. From the looks on their faces, she knew.

"He's dead, isn't he?" How could she say the words? Dead, what did that mean?

John shook his head. Dag cleared his throat. "We

hope not." He extended the letter bearing an official seal at the top.

Mary read it quickly, then went back to read each word one at a time. *We regret to inform you that Private First Class Willard Dunfey is missing in action and presumed dead.* The date was three months earlier.

Chapter
S I X

Then he isn't dead." Mary went to stand in front of the fire. She wanted to throw the horrible letter in and let the flames devour it.

"We can pray that he isn't," John said. He stepped closer and wrapped an arm around her shoulders.

"Father, wouldn't I know if Will no longer lived on this earth? I mean, he can't have been dead for three months and me not sense it, could he?"

"I don't know, child." John shook his head. "I just

don't know. The Almighty hasn't seen fit to let me know many things."

Mary looked up at her father. The lines had deepened in his face and his hair showed white all over. "What's been happening?"

"I had two funerals last week of boys shipped home to be buried. The oldest Gustafson boy and Teddy Bjorn. What can I say to those grieving parents—that this was God's will?"

He laid his cheek on the top of her head, now nestled against his shoulder. "I cannot say that war is God's will, that He is on the side of the right. He loves the Germans, too, not just the Americans and the English and French. We are all His children, so how can we go about killing each other?" His voice softened on the last words. "How?"

Mary felt the shudder that passed through him. Her gentle father, who loved all the children of the parish and their parents and relatives. Who never preached the fire and brimstone of other churches because he said God is love and His grace is made perfect in our human weakness. This man now had to bury the ones he loved, because of man's inhumanity to man.

But was war really human? She'd sat through many discussions and heard heart-stirring speeches about fighting for freedom, but did freedom have to come at the cost of so many lives? She had no answers, only questions.

Had Will really gone to his heavenly home, or was he on earth, suffering some unspeakable agony? If he were alive, wouldn't he have contacted her?

"You may have to accept the fact that he is gone." John drew his arms away and stepped back so he could see her face more clearly. "But not now!"

"No, not now."

Mary straightened her shoulders, reminiscent of

Mrs. Norgaard. She forced a smile to her quivering lips. "How is Daniel? And Mother with the Oiens? Did Mr. Oien give in yet and let Jenny have a kitty? She loves them so. How have you been? You're looking tired." Before he could answer, she turned to Dag, who had been sitting quietly. "How are Mrs. Norgaard and Clara?" Perhaps if she asked enough questions, the greater one would disappear.

"We are all fine," her father finally managed to insert. "In fact, with the cooler weather, Daniel has been doing well. Hasn't missed a day of school, but he would have today if he could have hidden out in my pocket to come along. He is counting the days until you come home for Christmas. Said to tell you he prays for Will every night."

That nearly undid her. She blinked several times and stared into the fire until she had herself under control. "Have you had supper?" When they shook their heads, she looked up at the carved clock on the mantel. "I'm sure Mrs. Killingsworth will let me fix you something in the kitchen. Where are you staying?"

"We aren't. We will catch the eleven o'clock back north. I just felt it important to give you this news in person, not through a letter or over the telephone."

Mary placed a hand on his arm. "Father, you are so kind. How lucky I am that I was born to you and Mor." She spun away before he could answer. "Let me check on supper for you."

An hour later she waved them on their way. "Thank you for coming along with him, Dag. You are a good friend."

He tipped his black, felt hat to her. "Mrs. Norgaard just wanted me to check up on her investment; this seemed as good a time as any." The twinkle in his eye let her know he was teasing.

"Well, then, since this was a business trip, thank

you for bringing my father along." She hugged her father one last time. "Pass that on to everyone, okay?"

She kept the smile in place as long as they looked back, but when she closed the door, the tears could no longer be held back. She stumbled against the lower step of the staircase and sat down. Leaning her head against the newel post, she couldn't have stopped the tears had she tried.

One by one the other young women in the boardinghouse came down the stairs and clustered around her. One offered a handkerchief; another went for a glass of water. Still another slipped into the music room and, sitting down at the piano, began playing the hymns they'd learned as children.

As the music washed over them, soon one began humming and then another.

When the storm of tears finally abated, Mary listened to the humming in harmony. Had a chorus of angels come just to give her strength? She closed her eyes and leaned against the post. They drifted from melody to melody as the pianist did, until she finally let the last notes drift away.

"Amen." As the notes died away, Janice took Mary's arm and tugged her to her feet. Together, arms around each other's waists, they climbed the stairs to the bedroom they shared.

"Thank you, all," Mary whispered. Talking loudly would have broken the spell.

When despair grabbed at her in the days to come, she remembered that peaceful music and the love of her friends. In spite of the official letter, each evening Mary added tales of the day to her own letters to Will. She continued to send them, refusing to allow herself to speculate about what was happening to them.

"I guess I'm afraid that if I quit, Will will be dead, and if I keep on, there's a chance he is alive," she explained to Janice one night. They'd been studying late because exams were coming up.

"How can you keep on going and not let it drag you down?" Janice tightened the belt of her flannel robe. "The not knowing—" She shook her head so her dark hair swung over one shoulder. She combed the tresses with her fingers and leaned back against the pillows piled at the head of her bed. "Makes me glad I don't have a sweetheart yet."

"I wouldn't trade my friendship and love for Will for all the men on campus."

"There are several who would ask if you gave them the chance."

"Janice!" Mary turned in her chair and locked her hands over the back. "I haven't treated any one of them as more than a friend."

"I know that. You act like you are already married,

for heaven's sake. I'm just telling you what I see. And hear."

"Oh, pooh, you're making that up." Mary turned back to her books. "Be quiet, I have to get this memorized."

But Mary recognized that her skirts hung looser about her waist and the shadows that lurked beneath her eyes grew darker, as if she hadn't enough sleep. Each night she committed Will to her heavenly Father's keeping and waved goodnight to him on the last star of the handle.

Two days before she left for home, she received a letter from her mother. *My dear Mary,* she read.

I have some sad news for you. Mrs. Oien, my dear friend Elizabeth, died from pneumonia two days ago. Dr. Harmon said she had no strength to fight it, and I could see that. I was with her when she breathed her last, as was Mr. Oien.

He is so broken up, I want to take him in my arms like I do Daniel, to comfort him. The funeral is tomorrow. The children are with us for the time being, as Kenneth can't seem to know what to do with them. He stayed home from work for the first day but said he was going crazy in that house without her.

The rest of us are eagerly waiting for your return. God keep you, my dear. Your loving mother.

Mary laid the paper in her lap and looked out the window into the blackness. A streetlight up by the corner cast a round circle of light on the freshly fallen snow. Clouds, pregnant with moisture, covered the twinkling stars. The night felt heavy, like the news in her lap.

"Oh, Elizabeth," Mary whispered, "how you must have fought to stay with your children. And your poor husband. Good-bye, my friend. Go with God." She sat down and wrote a letter of condolence to Mr. Oien, knowing she would get back to town nearly as soon as the letter but feeling she needed to write it anyway.

"What happened now?" Janice asked when she came in some time later.

Mary handed her the letter.

"Oh, that poor man." Janice looked up from her reading. "He'll need someone to care for his children." She tilted her head slightly sideways and looked at Mary. "You won't think you have to stay home next term and care for them?"

"No, I promised Mrs. Norgaard I would finish this

year. I just grew to care for Elizabeth so much last summer, and the children, Joey and Jenny, will be lost."

"Not if your mother has anything to do with it."

"Or Doc Harmon and Mrs. Norgaard. They'll probably have him married off in a month or two." Mary's smile slipped. "Men do that you know—marry again right away. I don't know how they can."

"For some I think marrying is like changing underwear. You do what's necessary."

"Janice Ringold!" Mary, feeling her jaw hit her chest, looked at her friend. The shock of the words made them both laugh. "You are outrageous, you know that?"

"I know. My mother always said my mouth would get me in trouble. 'Men don't like outspoken young ladies.' If I heard her say that once, I heard her a thousand times."

"Didn't help much, did it?" They chuckled again.

But before Mary fell asleep that night, she added an extra prayer for the Oien family along with her others, and as always, she gave Him Will.

·····

The house smelled like cinnamon and fresh-baked bread when Mary tiptoed in through the front door. Candles in the windows were ready to be lit on Christmas Eve, a pine tree from Minnesota filled the usual spot in the corner of the parlor, and garlands of cedar trimmed the doorway. Mary felt a pang; she'd missed the house decorating again. If only she'd had her last exam early in the week like many of the others, she could have left sooner. She could hear her mother in the kitchen, removing something from the oven.

Mary shut the door softly, hoping there would be no squeak, and when that was accomplished, she crossed the room to the kitchen. "Surprise!"

"Oh, my heavens!" Ingeborg grabbed at the sheet of

cookies that was headed for the floor. When she had the cookies safely on the table, she put her hand to her heart. "What are you trying to do, you naughty child, give your mother a heart attack?" But the smile that took in her whole face and her outstretched arms made light of her scolding words. "Land sakes, Mary, I didn't think you were ever coming."

A child's whimper came from the bedroom.

"Now see what you did—woke up Jenny. Joey won't be far behind."

"They are here?" Mary hugged her mother and began unwinding the bright red scarf about her neck. She hung it and then her coat on the rack by the door and reached outside for her valise. "You think they will remember me?"

"With Daniel telling them every day that Mary is coming, what do you think?" Ingeborg cocked her head and listened. "I think she'll settle down again. Give us time for a cup of coffee and some catching up."

"I have another box at the station; it was too heavy to carry."

"Mary, you didn't spend your money on Christmas presents, did you?"

"Some, and some I made, like always. There are some books there for my classroom—when I get a classroom, that is." She sat down at the table and watched her mother take down the good china cups. They only came down for special company and the Ladies' Aid. Ingeborg set the one with tiny rosebuds around the rim in front of her daughter. It had been her favorite since when she was little and they had tea once in a great while.

Oh, I'm home, Mary thought. *I never know how much I miss it and my family until I come back. But this time there will be no Will to come sweep me off my feet.* She sighed. A bit of the sunlight went out of the day. *You knew better,* she scolded herself. *You knew he wasn't here, so behave yourself. Don't take your feelings out on Mor, who is so happy to see you.*

After Ingeborg poured the coffee, she took her daughter's chin in gentle fingers and tilted her face toward the light. "Have you been sick?"

Mary shook her head.

"Working too hard and not sleeping enough?" She tilted the girl's head down and kissed the forehead. "Grieving for Will?" Her words were soft as the ashes falling in the stove.

"Oh, Mor." Mary flung her arms around her mother's waist and buried her face in the flour-dusted apron. "I can't believe he's dead. Wouldn't I know, some part of me down in my heart? Wouldn't I know for sure?"

Ingeborg stroked the soft curls and brushed the wisps of hair back that framed Mary's face. "I've heard tell of that, of mothers with their children, sometimes

of those who've been married for many years, but—"
She bent down and laid her cheek on Mary's head. "My
dear, I just don't know."

They stayed that way, comforting each other for a
time. Finally Mary drew away.

Ingeborg brushed some flour off her daughter's
cheek. "Now the coffee is gone cold. Let me heat it up."
She poured the brown liquid back in the pot and set it
on the front burner again. "One thing I do know. When
the time comes, you say good-bye, knowing that you
loved him and he loved you and love goes on forever.
But Will wouldn't want you to grieve overlong; he'd
want you to get on with your life."

"I'll be teaching next year. Isn't that getting on with
my life?"

"Ja, it is. God, I know, has special plans for you, and
when we cry, He says He is right here with us. As He is
all the time."

Mary watched the peace on her mother's face and heard the faith in her voice. Ingeborg's faith never wavered. Could she ever be strong like that?

⁕

"Mary's home!" The cry rang through the house when school let out and the children ran in through the door. Jenny and Joey came out of their rooms, rubbing their eyes, and after a moment, joined the others in the circle around Mary. Everyone talked at once until the ceiling echoed with happy laughter.

Supper that night continued in the same vein. When Mr. Oien came to pick up his children, Ingeborg invited him to stay for a bite to eat. They pulled out the table and set in another leaf so there would be room.

Once or twice his smiles at the antics of the younger Moen children nearly reached his eyes. "Thank you so much," he said as he readied to leave after the meal was finished.

"You're welcome to stay longer." John leaned back in his chair and crossed his legs at the ankles.

"I...I'd best be going—put these two to bed, you know." He nodded toward Joey and Jenny, who were being bundled up by the Moens. "Again, thank you." He put his hat on and picked up Jenny. "Come, Joey." He took the boy's hand, and the three went down the walk to where he had parked his automobile at the front gate.

"He should have started that contraption first." Ingeborg shut the door and peeked through the lace curtain. "Knute, why don't you go out and help him crank that thing?"

The oldest Moen son did as asked. When he returned, he rubbed his hands together. "If it weren't for cranking those things, I'd want one the worst way."

"Wanting never hurt anyone." John winked at Mary.

"I was hoping since you were home, you would read to us tonight."

"Of course. What are you reading?" She took the book her father handed her. "Oh, Charles Dickens and old Scrooge. How I love it." As soon as the dishes were washed and put away, the family gathered in the parlor and Mary began to read. After the chapter was finished, she picked up the Bible that lay on the end table and opened it to the Psalms. "I keep going back to this one. 'Oh Lord, thou has searched me, and known me.'"

"Psalm 139." Daniel beamed at being the first to recognize it. They'd played this game of guessing the Scripture all the years of their lives, until now they were all well-versed in Bible knowledge.

Mary continued reading and, when she finished, closed the book. "Far, will you pray tonight?"

John nodded. "Father in heaven, Thou dost indeed know us right well. We ask You to forgive us our sins and fill us with Your Holy Spirit so that we may do the works Thou hast given us." When he came to the end, he finished with a blessing and they all said, "Amen."

"Now I know I am home for sure," Mary said with a sigh and a smile.

She felt that same way in church a few nights later when they gathered to celebrate the birth of the Christ child. Singing the old hymns and hearing the words embedded in her memory from eighteen Christmases made her want to wrap her arms around every person in the room. *Please, God, if You will, send me a sign that Will is either here on earth or up there with You. I want to do Your will, and I thank You that You sent Your Son to walk this earth. All I ask, dear Father, is a small sign.*

Christmas passed in a blur of happiness, only saddened when Mary thought of Will and what he was missing. Two days later, Dag came to see them.

"I have something that came in the mail today." He stopped, swallowed hard, and continued.

Mary felt an icy hand grip her heart.

Dag held out something metal on his hand. "They say these are Will's dog tags, taken from a body buried in Germany."

Mary couldn't breathe.

Chapter
SEVEN

"Mary, are you all right?"

She heard the voice as if from a great distance. "I...I'm fine. Why?" Had she been sitting in the chair when...? Memory crashed back and she whimpered. "No, no, please no." *Dear God, please, that's not the sign I wanted. I know I asked for a sign but...*

Dag stood before her, his hand clenched at his side, a small piece of chain dangling between thumb and forefinger.

Now, why would I notice something like that? Chains don't matter at this point. But that one did. The chain that Will had worn so proudly now brought agony to his beloved.

"Mary." Her father's face swam before her eyes. He cradled her cold hands in his warm ones and waited for her to respond.

"Yes." She left off studying the shimmering hairs on the backs of his hands and looked at him. The tears fighting to overflow his blue eyes undid her. She threw herself into his arms and wept.

Minutes later but what seemed like hours—she accepted the handkerchief from her mother and mopped at her eyes. "I wanted him to come home. I asked God, and you said God always answers our prayers. I prayed that He would bring Will home."

"I know. I did, too."

"And me." Dag lowered himself into a chair and leaned forward. "All of us prayed for that."

"Then why?" She shouted her question, shaking her fist in the face of God. "Why did He let Will die? Others are coming home why not Will?"

John bent his head. "I don't know. I do not understand the mind of God or some of His purposes. All I know is that His heart breaks, too, and He holds us close. Close like me holding your hand and even closer. And the other thing I know with all certainty is that you will see Will again."

"I know about heaven, but I want him here." Tears dripped down her face.

"I know that, too."

Mary felt her mother's hands on her shoulders, warm and secure.

"God could have saved Will." Again she felt like lashing out.

"Ja, He could have." The hands on her shoulders rubbed gently.

"Then why didn't He?" Mary hiccupped on the last word.

"I 'spect every wife, mother, friend, feels the same. None of us want someone we love to be killed." John rubbed the back of her hands with his thumbs.

"Am I being selfish?"

"No more'n anyone else. But death comes. It is part of life, and we look forward to heaven all the time."

Mary sat silently. Then she shook her head. "It's not fair. Will is such a good man."

"Yes, he was. You can be proud he was your friend and loved you with all his heart."

It bothered her that her father said "was." She couldn't think of Will as "was." *He is!* Her rebellious mind insisted. *Will is.*

When she awoke in the middle of the night, after

alternately praying and crying, she found her mother sitting by the bed, sound asleep. Mary fought back tears again. This was so like her mother, keeping watch over those she loved and those who needed her. Her presence comforted the girl, and she drifted back to sleep.

Each day felt like she waded through spring gumbo three feet deep. Every part of her felt heavy, even to her eyelids and the tops of her ears. She pushed her hair back and finally braided it and coiled the braid in a bun at the base of her head to keep the weight of it from pulling her over. All she really wanted to do was sleep, for only in sleep did the knowledge disappear. But on waking, it always returned. They said Will was dead.

"You can stay home, you know." Ingeborg helped

fold the under-garments to put in Mary's traveling valise.

"Would it be any better?" Mary turned from sorting through her books and deciding which had to go back with her.

"It would for me, because then I could make sure you eat and get enough rest and—"

"And cluck over me like one of your chicks?"

"You are one of my chicks." Ingeborg smoothed a ribbon into place on a nightgown. "No matter how grown-up you get—even when you have a family of your own—you will always be my eldest chick."

"But I have to grow up, and learning to keep going is part of that, isn't it?"

"Ja, and I know our heavenly Father will watch over you and keep you safe."

I hope He does a better job with me than He did with Will. Mary was horrified at her thoughts. They just snuck up on her and dashed off before she could rope them in and discipline them to behave.

Later, her bags all packed, Mary bundled up to walk over to the mansion to say good-bye to Mrs. Norgaard. The north wind bit her cheeks and tried to burrow into her bones.

"Come in, my dear, come in." Clara swung the door wide open. "Are you about frozen clear through, out walking in this cold?" Mary stamped the snow from her boots and smiled at the diminutive dynamo in front of her. Clara Weinlander often reminded Mary of her mother. If there was something that needed doing, those two women would take it on.

"Herself is waiting for you." Mrs. Hanson secretly used that nickname for her employer, and at times, so did half the town. "We'll bring the coffee right in."

After their greetings, Mrs. Norgaard beckoned Mary to sit beside her on the sofa in front of the south windows. "I want to say something to you before the others come in."

Mary sat and turned to face her benefactress. "Yes."

"Losing one you love is one of the hardest things in life, but there's something I learned through all that. The Bible says, 'This too shall pass,' and it will. Right now you doubt me, but in a few weeks, months, the pain will be less and there will be some days when you surprise yourself because you didn't think of missing him at all."

Gudrun covered Mary's hands with her own. "Trust me, child, I know it is true. And one day you will think of Will, and the memory will be sweet. For you see, he will be closer now than he could have been when he was alive."

Mary felt the tears burning and closed her eyes. "But...but I still feel he might be alive, somewhere, somehow."

"I know, the mind plays tricks like that on us. Oh, how often I thought my husband would be home in half an hour. But he was gone, and finally I came to accept that. And that's when I began to live again." She looked up to see Clara and Mrs. Hanson with the serving trays. "And much of that is thanks to these two. They bullied me into wanting to live."

"That we did." Mrs. Hanson set the tray down. "And would again."

"Just think of all the exciting things you would have missed." Clara sat in the chair and leaned forward to pour the coffee from the silver pot. "Mary, help yourself to those cookies. Mrs. Hanson baked them just for you, and there's a box for you to take with you."

In spite of herself, Mary left the mansion feeling a little less weighed down by life.

With papers to write and new classes, Mary found

herself busier than ever. Her friends gathered round her and made sure she ate and went with them to the lectures on campus to hear the suffragettes trying to get the suffrage bill passed through Congress. When it was defeated, they all held a wake.

When General Pershing made his triumphant entrance into Paris, they all listened to the speeches on the radio in the parlor. Surely peace would be coming soon.

But the war continued, and school drew to a close. The entire Moen tribe came down on the train for Mary's graduation from normal school. She would now be able to teach grades one through high school in the state of North Dakota. Mary almost, but not quite, kept from looking for Will in the well-wishers.

"To think, a daughter of mine has graduated from teaching school." Ingeborg clasped her hands at her waist.

"I won't be the last." Mary removed the square black mortar board that crowned her head. "I will help pay for the next one who wants to go. Has Knute talked about what he wants to do?" Her brother next in line was due to graduate from high school at the end of May. She looked down at the brother tugging on her arm. "Yes, Daniel?"

"Far said if you were to change, we could go have ice cream."

"Oh, he did, did he? Well, let me congratulate my friends over there, and we will all walk to the soda fountain."

"I think we need a place like this in Soldahl," Ingeborg said after they took their places in two adjoining booths.

"That's right, Mother, you need something else to do." Mary shook her head.

"I didn't say I should do it." She looked around at the

scroll-backed metal chairs and the small round tables. "But think what—"

"Don't even think such a thing." John leaned across the table to bring his face closer to his wife's. "You have far too much to do right now."

"Well."

"Mother!" Mary couldn't tell if her mother was serious or just teasing. After the young man took their order, Ingeborg leaned back against the high-backed wooden bench and turned to her daughter. "So, how are you, really?" She studied Mary's face, searching for the truth.

"I am much better. Mrs. Norgaard was right. Only by looking back can I tell how far I've come. I'm not angry at God anymore—or anyone else. I can read His Word and let it bless me again. But I still write my letters every night to Will and collect them in a box. I guess that has become my diary." She didn't tell them of not looking for the Big Dipper anymore. She still had a hard time looking up at the night sky at all. Invariably when she did, her eyes filled with tears and she couldn't make out the stars anyway.

"I could tell a difference in your letters. Your father and I want you to know how proud we are of you."

The sodas arrived, and the conversation turned to how good they tasted and what everyone was planning for the summer.

"Mr. Oien has been writing and asking if I would care for the children again this summer."

"I know," Ingeborg responded. "I think he sees that with all of my own children home, his two little ones might be too much."

"He doesn't know you very well then, does he?" Mary sipped on her straw. Her mother's straw hat had just been knocked askew by an arm belonging to one of the boys, who had been reaching over the back of the bench. Mary gave the hand a pinch and smiled at the "yeow" that her action provoked. Her mother righted the hat with a laugh and a threat to fix the perpetrator good. The booth full of children laughed at her words, knowing their mother would get even somehow, sometime when they least expected it.

Mary felt a glow settle about her heart. How she had missed them, mostly without even knowing it.

"So what will you do?" Ingeborg finally asked.

"I will care for his house and children and keep on searching for my school. I have my application in four different places, so time will tell."

"And that is what you want?"

Mary nodded. "This is what I want. Since God made sure I got through school, He must have a place in mind for me."

But the summer passed swiftly, and still Mary hadn't heard. By the end of August, she had a hard time keeping doubts at bay. Would she get a school? If not,

what would she do?

Chapter

EIGHT

The letter arrived on a Wednesday. Mary stared at the postmark, then slit open the envelope with a shaking finger. Grafton lay in the next township, but the school they mentioned was not in town. If they hired her, she would be teaching first through fourth at a country school with two classrooms. Could she come for an interview on Friday?

Could she come for an interview? Did cows give milk? Did the moon follow the sun? An interview! She finally had an interview. And she wouldn't be clear on the other side of the state. She could see the dear faces of her family on the weekends—that is, if she could afford the train. She hurried home to share her news.

Questions bubbled to the surface. Where would she live? Oh, not with a family that made her share a room and bed with one of their children. Sometimes that was the arrangement. In some places families still took turns boarding the teacher. She'd heard some terrible stories about situations like that. Her feet slowed. If only she could teach right here in Soldahl.

"Mary, that is wonderful." Ingeborg clasped her hands in delight. "And so close by."

Mary read the letter out loud, the actual sound of the words making it more of a reality. "So, will you care for the children on Friday for me?" she asked her mother.

"Of course. You must call the people in Grafton

and tell them what time your train will arrive. This is late for hiring a new teacher. I wonder what happened there? I hope it was not an illness of the teacher they already had."

Or she didn't want to go back and found a position elsewhere. Mary shook her head. Thoughts like that were better barricaded behind steel doors.

On Friday, Mary boarded the early train and returned home in time for supper, the proud owner of a teaching position. She would report for duty in two weeks in order to have her classroom ready for her pupils.

"So, why did they need a teacher at this late date?" Ingeborg asked after the children were all in bed.

"Miss Brown's mother became ill in Minnesota and she had to go be with her. A man teaches the older grades—has for a long time. I will be staying with a widow about a mile from the schoolhouse and helping her in exchange for board. I met with her, and she seems very nice. She's a bit hard of hearing and speaks German as much as English, but we should do fine."

"Anyone who has you to help them is very blessed indeed. Helping doesn't mean milking cows and such, does it?" Ingeborg wiped her hands on her apron. "You never have had to do farm labor."

"If you ask me, her sons just want someone living with their mother. She said she didn't want to go live with them." Mary's eyes danced. "I think she doesn't want anyone bossing her around." She caught her mother by the hands and whirled around the kitchen with her. "Oh, Mr. Gunderson, the head of the school board, told me three times that they didn't want any fooling around. 'Our teachers must be a model of decorum.'" She deepened her voice to mimic the gentleman. "Mother, this is the twentieth century for pity's sake. He must still be back in the Dark Ages."

"So what did you tell him?"

Mary's smile slipped. "I told him my fiancé was killed in the war and all I was interested in was teaching children the three Rs."

The next afternoon when Mr. Oien came home from work, Mary gave him her good news.

"I'm so very happy for you," he said, but his face showed shock and what was it—bewilderment?

"You knew I planned on teaching school if I could find a position?"

"I did. But since you hadn't said anything, I'd hoped you would stay." He sank down in a chair by the door.

"My mother will watch the children again." Mary stepped to the window to check on the two who were playing outside in the sandbox. They were so sweet, and she would indeed miss them.

"That is not the problem." He paused, then continued in a rush. "I had not planned to mention this yet, what with your grieving for Will and all, but you love my children and you are so good with them and you are such a lovely person, and would you consider marrying me?"

"What did you say?"

"I asked you to marry me." He smoothed his sandy hair back with his hands. A smile came to his face. "I did it. I asked you to marry me."

"But you don't love me."

"How do you know? I love having you here with Joey and Jenny when I come home. I love seeing you play with them. I love hearing you laugh and I—"

"But I don't love you," Mary said the words softly, gently.

"You could, you know. I make a good living, you wouldn't have to teach school, you'd be near to your family whom I know you love dearly, you would have a nice house, and..."

Mary's slow shaking of the head forced him to run down.

"Please," he quickly amended, "don't say no right now. Give it some thought. Let me visit you, take you for drives. We could have a picnic— a...a..."

Mary stared at him. The thought of marrying someone other than Will brought a knot to her throat and tears to her eyes. "I have to go. Thank you for... for—" She turned and bolted out the door.

<hr />

"What happened to you?" Ingeborg's eyes widened when she saw her daughter's face.

"He.... he asked me to m-marry him." Mary put a hand to her throat.

"A bit of a surprise, that?" Ingeborg shook her head. "Well, I never." She stirred the kettle simmering on the stove. "Hmm, that idea has possibilities."

"Possibilities! Mother, I don't love Kenneth."

"Yet. Sometimes the best marriages are when two people grow into love."

"Mother! You want me to marry someone I don't love?"

"I didn't say that. But I can see it is a natural choice from his point of view. You are lovely, you are familiar, you know his home, and you love his children. Many men would say that's more than enough basis for marriage. Women have married for a lot less, you know."

Mary felt like she was talking with a total stranger who somehow wore her mother's face. "I don't think I have any more to say to you." She turned on her heel and climbed the stairs to her bedroom. Flinging herself across her bed, she buried her face in her hands. *Oh, Will, why did you have to go and die?*

Time took wings during the days until Mary left,

making her breathless most of the time. So much to be finished. In spite of her feelings of misgivings, she continued to care for Joey and Jenny, bringing them back to her mother's on the afternoons when she had errands to run.

She wanted her classroom just perfect for her new pupils and spent hours preparing calendars and pictures, lesson assignments, and flash cards for numbers. Mr. Gunderson had said the school didn't have a large budget for supplies—the year had been hard for the farmers, in spite of the high prices for grain due to the war.

Mrs. Norgaard insisted that Dag would drive Mary to her new home so she wouldn't have to take all her things on the train. "God will be with you, child, as you share His love for those children. Don't you forget it."

"I'm not about to." Mary gave the old woman a hug. "You take care of yourself now while I'm away."

"Humph." Gudrun straightened her back, as if it needed it. "I've been taking care of myself since before your mother and father were born. I surely won't stop now." But the twinkle in her faded blue eyes turned the tear that shimmered on her lashes brilliant. She waved one slender hand. "You drive careful now, Dag, you hear?"

Clara, too, stood in the doorway, waving them off. "We'll keep supper for you, Dag. Enjoy the day."

"I wish she could have come." Mary settled back in her seat. The wind whipped the scarf she'd tied around her hat and blew the ends straight out behind her. The thrill of driving such speeds! *One day,* she promised herself, *I will have a car of my own to drive.* The picture of the black roadster driven by Kenneth Oien flashed through her mind. What would it be like, married to him? She liked him well enough. In fact, they could probably be friends. She shrugged the thoughts away.

He'd said he'd write and gladly drive up to bring her home for a weekend. She deliberately pushed the thoughts out of her mind.

"So, how goes the blacksmithing?" She turned in the seat so Dag could hear her above the roar of the automobile and the rushing wind.

"Slow. I know I will have to convert more and more to repairing tractors and automobiles and trucks. With the engines improving all the time, we will see more changes than we ever dreamed of."

"I agree." She sought for another topic, but let it lie. Talking above the noise took too great an effort.

Dag carried all her boxes into the schoolroom, and then took the suitcases into the Widow Williamson's two-story square farmhouse and up the stairs to the large bedroom facing east. When he straightened, his head brushed the slanted ceiling, so he ducked a bit.

"This is very nice."

"I think so." Mrs. Williamson had even brought up a desk and chair to set in front of the window. Carved posts stood above a white bedspread, and extra pillows nearly hid the oak headboard. Braided rag rugs by the bed and in front of the high dresser would keep Mary's feet off cold floors in the winter, and there was more than enough space for her simple wardrobe in the double-doored oak chifforobe. A picture of Jesus the Shepherd hung by the door.

"Well, I'd best be on my way." Dag extended his hand. "You call if you need anything. I saw a telephone on the wall downstairs."

"Thank you for all your help." Mary walked him down the stairs, turning at the landing and on down. When his car roared to life and he drove away, she stood on the porch waving long after the dust had settled. She was on her own now—just what she had always wanted. Or had she?

Mary fell in love with her pupils the instant they shuffled through the door. She had sixteen all together: four in the first grade, all so shy they couldn't look up at her; three in the second; five in the third; and four in fourth. The fourth graders already bossed the younger ones, but when she rapped for order, they all sat at attention.

"We will stand for the flag salute." She checked her seating chart. "Arnold, will you lead us?" She put her hand over her pounding heart. Were they as nervous as she? She nodded at the boy on the outside row.

"I pledge allegiance to the flag..." They stumbled through the words, some having forgotten them and others having not yet learned.

One of the first graders broke into tears when Mary asked them to repeat the Lord's Prayer. And when they sang the "Star Spangled Banner," she mostly sang solo. These children had a lot to learn.

She had planned on standing in front of them and quizzing them on their reading and numbers, but at the sight of the tears, she called all the children to the side of the room and, sitting down on a chair, told them to sit in front of her. She smiled at each one when she called their names again.

"I need to know who you are, so could you please tell me something you like to do?"

The older children looked at each other wide-eyed.

"Arnold, we'll start with you. What do you like?" And so she went around the group, and by the time she reached the youngest ones, they smiled back at her. One little towheaded girl stared at her teacher with her heart in her eyes.

"You are so pretty," she whispered. "I like you."

Mary felt her heart turn over. "And I like you." She laid the tip of her finger on the little girl's button nose.

"Now, let's all learn the pledge of allegiance because we are going to start every day saluting our flag."

"My brother went to war for our flag." One of the boys said. "He never comed home."

Mary knew she was going to have heart problems for certain. "That has happened to many of our young men, so when we salute the flag, we are remembering them at the same time." Thoughts of a star in the Big Dipper handle twinkled through her mind. Remembering. Yes, the sweetness promised by Mrs. Norgaard had finally come.

"A very dear friend of mine went to Europe to fight, too, and never came home." She laid a hand on the head of a little boy who had gravitated next to her knee. "Now, repeat after me, I pledge allegiance to the flag..." And so the morning continued. By the time recess came around, Mary felt like running outside to play with the children.

"The first day is always the hardest." Mr. Colburn, his graying hair worn long over the tops of his ears, stood in her doorway. His kind brown eyes and smile that made his mustache wiggle invited her to smile back.

"Is that a promise?" Mary stretched her shoulders. "Mr. Colburn, everyone spoke so highly of you, I feel honored to share your building."

"Yes, well, I try, and the honor is mine. I think we will do well together. My wife insisted I bring you home for supper one night soon. She is so curious about the new teacher, I made her promise not to come see you for herself. We've lived here for ten years, and we are still not considered part of the community. She's hoping you can be friends."

"Isn't that nice? I never turn down the offer of friendship."

"I'll go ring the bell." Mr. Colburn left, and

immediately the bell in the tower bonged twice. The children flew to form a line starting with the larger ones and going to the smallest and marched into the building.

Mary took a deep breath and dove back in.

The days fell into a pattern. Up before dawn to make breakfast while Mrs. Williamson did the outside chores. Then walk to school, teach all day, and walk home. Evenings, after she'd washed the supper dishes, were spent preparing for the next day. On Saturday they cleaned house, and on Sunday, Mrs. Williamson's sons took turns driving them to church.

Mary didn't have time to be lonely. She continued to write her letters to Will each night, but now she planned to send them to her mother. Ingeborg would love to hear the stories of her daughter and her small charges.

When Mr. Colburn discovered she could play the

piano, he rolled the heavy instrument into her room on the condition that she teach music. The students at Valley School loved to sing. So every afternoon, if all had done their assignments, everyone gathered in Mary's classroom for singing and then Mr. Colburn read to them. His mellow voice played the parts as he read first *The Jungle Book*, by Rudyard Kipling, and then *Oliver Twist*, by Charles Dickens. Mary was as entranced as the children.

Letters came weekly from Kenneth Oien, and Mary grew to look forward to them. While she had yet to go home to visit, his letters were like a window into the life of Soldahl. He wrote of the antics of Joey and Jenny and their new friend, Mews, a half-grown cat that had shown up on their doorstep one day. He described the changing of the colors with the frost and the geese flying south. He said they all missed her and looked forward to her coming home.

There's a poet hiding in that man's soul, Mary thought as she read the latest letter. *But can I ever think of him as more than a friend?*

When the telephone rang one evening and Mrs. Williamson called up the stairs to say it was for her, Mary felt her heart leap into her throat. Was something wrong at home? Was Daniel sick again?

"Hello?" She knew she sounded breathless, only because she was.

"Mary, this is Kenneth."

"Kenneth? Oh, Mr. Oien...uh, Kenneth." She felt like an idiot. Surely they could be on a first-name basis by now, in fact should have been a long time ago.

"I wondered if I could come and get you on Friday afternoon, if you would like to come home, that is. I would take you back on Sunday, after church. I...ah, that is—"

Mary took pity on his stammering. "I would love that. Thank you for the invitation."

"Would you like me to come to the school?"

"No, I'll meet you here at Mrs. Williamson's." She gave him the directions and hung the ear piece back on the hook. She'd heard a click on the party line. Now everyone around would know the new teacher had a beau. Whether he was or not did not matter.

"I think of you a lot," Kenneth said when he stopped the automobile in front of the parsonage that Friday night. Dark had fallen before they reached Soldahl, and traveling the rough roads by lamplight had made them drive even more slowly.

What could she say? "I enjoy reading your letters. And thank you for the ride home. Will you be coming to dinner on Sunday?"

"Yes." He smiled at her in the dimness. "And we have

been invited to supper on Saturday at the mansion. That is, if you would like to go."

"Why, of course." Mary fumbled for her purse. "Thank you again for the ride."

He got out and came around to open her door, leaving the motor running. "Till tomorrow then." He helped her out and carried her valise to the door. "Jenny and Joey hope you will come see them while you are in town."

"Oh." Mary wondered what had happened to her tongue. Suffering from a lack of words was a new experience for her.

Looking back, she couldn't remember having a nicer time in a long while. While she was fully aware that all her friends and family were playing matchmakers, she couldn't fault them for it. Kenneth Oien was a very nice man.

But a few weeks later, when he asked her to consider marriage, she shook her head.

"Please don't pressure me," she whispered. "I just cannot answer that yet."

"Yet?" His eager voice came through the darkness. He'd just brought her back from another weekend at home. He touched her cheek with a gentle caress.

Mary held herself still. If that had been Will, the urge to throw herself in his arms would have made her shake. All she felt was a longing to feel more. What was the matter with her?

Chapter

NINE

The world went crazy on Tuesday, November 11, 1918. Victory Day. The war to end all wars was over. School bells rang, radio announcers shouted, the people cheered. Some sobbed at the thought their sons might still make it home in one piece. Others cried for those who would never return.

Mary was one of the latter. While her head said, "Thank You, Father, for finally bringing peace," her heart cried for the young man she had seen leave for war.

While the children were out on the playground after eating their lunches, she walked out beyond the coal shed and leaned against the building wall. Letting the tears come, she sobbed until she felt wrung out. When she could finally feel the cold wind biting her cheeks and tugging at her hair, she wiped her eyes and lifted her face to the sun that played hide-and-seek in the clouds.

"Will," she whispered, "I loved you then and I love you now, but I guess it is about time I got on with my life. One more Christmas is all I will ask for, and then if God wants me to marry Kenneth Oien, I will follow His bidding." She waited, almost hoping for an answer, but all she heard was the wind and it was too light to look for that star.

Kenneth and the children joined the Moens for

Thanksgiving dinner after the church service. Pastor Moen had thanked God for bringing peace to a world torn asunder by war, and the congregation heartily agreed. Mary refused to let the tears come again. She sat in the front pew but didn't dare look directly up at her father, for she knew the love in his eyes would be her undoing. Why was it always so hard to keep from crying in church?

Several of the boys, now turned men, had returned from the service already, making it easy for some families to give thanks. One even brought back a French wife, and if that didn't start the gossips buzzing...

Mary felt sorry for the shy young woman. If only she could speak French to help her out.

They had stuffed goose for dinner, two given them by one of the hunters in the congregation. Ingeborg had been cooking for a week, or so the amount of food on the table testified. Afterward they played charades, and when the two little ones woke up from their naps, they played hide the thimble. Jenny ignored the game and came to sit on Mary's lap, leaning her head back against Mary's chest.

Mary looked up to catch a glance between her parents. *Please, don't push me,* she wanted to cry. Cuddling Jenny was so easy. Would cuddling with her father be as simple?

"You know, Kenneth is a fine young man," John said after the company had left.

"Yes, Father, I know you like him." Mary bit off the colored thread she was using to embroider a rose on a handkerchief for Mrs. Williamson. Making Christmas presents had begun.

"He will make a fine husband," Ingeborg said without looking up from her knitting.

"All right. I know how you feel and I know how he feels. All I want to know now is how God feels."

"And what about you?" John kept his finger in his place in the book. "How do you feel?"

"Like I cannot make a decision yet."

John nodded. "You don't have to."

"I want to go through Christmas first. I will make a decision after the first of the year. Then it will have been a year since we got the final word. But I know one thing for sure, no matter what my decision, I will finish my year at Valley School."

John and Ingeborg both nodded. Daniel wandered back down the stairs, rubbing the sleep out of his eyes. "I heard you talking, and it made me hungry."

Mary laughed as she rose to cut him another piece of pumpkin pie. "You should be as big as Knute with all that you eat."

The weeks before Christmas passed in a blur of preparing a school program and party for the families around Pleasant Valley. They decorated a Christmas tree someone brought from Minnesota and hung chains made from colored paper around the room. But the music made Mary the most proud. The children sang like the angels had from on high, and during the performance even the most stoic fathers dabbed at their eyes more than once.

Mary left for home with her presents completed and bearing treasures given her by her students. Her favorite, if she were allowed to pick, was a card decorated with pressed wildflowers and lettered, "To my teechur."

A snowstorm hung on the northern horizon, so she took the train, rather than allowing Dag or Kenneth to come for her. While it would take a lot of snow to stop the train, automobiles buried themselves in drifts with the ease of children finding a mud puddle.

Her father met her at the station with his horse and

buggy. He took her valise and wrapped an arm around her shoulders. "Do you have anything more?"

"Father, at Christmas?" Her laugh pealed out. She pointed to two boxes tied up tightly with twine. "Those are mine. What happened to all the fancy automobiles?"

"Too much snow." John loaded the boxes into the area behind the seat and helped her up. "I sure hope we don't have a blizzard for Christmas."

She told him about the school program on the way home, her arm tucked in his and a robe covering their knees. When her story finished, she said, "You know one good thing about horses?"

"No, what's that?"

"You can talk and hear the other person answer." She leaned closer to him. "Without shouting."

"I know. Sometimes I think if the congregation offered me an automobile, I'd turn it down." He slapped the reins, clucking the gray gelding into a trot. "General, here, and I, we've been through a lot together. An automobile won't take me home if I fall asleep after a late call or listen to me practice my sermon. If he doesn't like one, he shakes his head and snorts. Then I know I need to go back to the desk and keep writing."

Big white flakes drifted before the wind, glistening and dancing in the streetlights. Two days until Christmas. This year they could truly say peace on earth and goodwill to men.

They spent the next two days baking *julekake*, the Norwegian Christmas bread, *sandbaklse*, and *krumkake* and frying *fatigman* and rosettes. The house smelled of nutmeg and cardamom, pine and cedar. No one was allowed to open a door without knocking or peek into closets or on shelves.

Ingeborg spent the late hours of Christmas Eve afternoon at the stove beating the *rommegrote*, until the melted butter from the cream rose to the surface to make a rich pudding. If anyone tried to sneak tastes, she batted them away with her wooden spoon. "If you want some, you'll have to wait or make your own." She'd been saying the same thing every year that Mary could remember.

When they finally trooped off on the walk to church, Mary stayed in the midst of her family. Kenneth finally sat in a pew a few behind them, a look of puzzlement on his face.

With Daniel glued to one side and Beth, her youngest sister, on the other, Mary put her arms around them and let them hold the hymnal. She didn't need to see the words; she'd known the carols all her life. And for a change she could sit with her family since other people now played the piano and organ Mrs. Norgaard had donated two years earlier. The music swelled, and the congregation joined in. "Silent night, holy night, all is calm, all is bright."

Two people stood to read the Christmas story. "And it came to pass in those days..."

Mary could say the words along with the readers. "And they laid the babe in the manger for there was no room for them in the inn."

A hush fell as Reverend John stepped into the pulpit. He stood there, head bowed.

Mary heard a stir in the back but kept her eyes on her father. When he raised his head, he gasped. He looked to Mary and then to the back of the room.

The buzz grew with people shifting and murmuring.

Mary turned and looked over her shoulder.

The man coming up the center aisle walked as if he knew the way. Well he should. He'd helped lay the carpet.

He stopped at the end of the pew. "Hello, Mary. Merry Christmas."

"Will." She rose to her feet. Her gaze melded with

his. Her heart stopped beating and then started again, triple-time. She shifted so there was room for him to sit beside her. Hands clamped as if they'd never let go, they raised their faces to the man standing openmouthed in the pulpit.

"Dearly beloved," John's voice broke. He blew his nose and tucked his handkerchief up the sleeve of his robe. "I'm sorry, folks, but never have those words been more true." He wiped his eyes with the back of his hand. "We have been given an extraordinary gift, as you all know. Welcome home, Will Dunfey."

Mary heard no more of the sermon. *Will is alive! Thank You, God, thank You.* Over and over the words repeated in her mind. Tears ran unchecked down her cheeks, and while her chin quivered, she couldn't quit smiling. Not that she wanted to.

When the benediction sounded, she rose along with the others. At the final amen, when the organ poured out its triumphal notes, she turned to Will and melted into his arms. Proper or no, the kiss they shared spoke of all their heartache and all their joy. Will Dunfey had come home.

"It was my destiny," he said later after he'd shaken every hand and been clapped on the back a hundred times by all the congregation. He and Mary were sitting in the parlor at the parsonage with all the Moens, the Weinlanders, and Mrs. Norgaard. "I told Mary I would come home, and Dag taught me to always keep my word."

A chuckle rippled through the room.

"Where were you?" Daniel held the place of honor at Will and Mary's feet.

"In a prisoner-of-war camp. I lost my dog tags, and for a long time I didn't know who I was. I've been trying to get home ever since the signing of the peace. They kept me in a hospital for a while, then told me I was dead." He raised his left hand, leaving his right hand still holding firmly on to Mary's. "I said I might have been, but I was alive now and my name was still Willard Dunfey."

Mary laid her head on his shoulder. "Everyone insisted you were dead, but my heart didn't believe it. I thought I was going crazy, so I asked God for a sign and a couple of days later, your dog tags arrived."

"When that happened, we were sure they had buried you over there." Mrs. Norgaard took a lace handkerchief from the edge of her sleeve and wiped her eyes again. "Must be something in the air."

"Of course," Dag managed to say with a straight face.

"They would have except for this." Will took the Testament Mary had given him from his shirt pocket and held it up. A hole showed through the upper half.

"Good God," John breathed.

"It slowed the bullet so it couldn't penetrate my ribs. I bled like a stuck pig, but flesh wounds heal. So you see, Mary, you saved my life."

"The Word of God is powerful in more ways than one." Gudrun wiped her eyes again. "Pesky cold."

Later when everyone else had gone home or gone to bed, Mary and Will put on their coats and stepped out on the porch. The storm had blown over, and the stars shone like crystals against the black sky. Will pointed to the end of the Dipper.

"You don't need to look for me up there anymore because I am right here, and here I will stay. My love for you has only grown deeper, your face kept me from ever giving up, and," he patted his chest, "I have a scar to remind me how close I came to losing you."

Mary laid her hand over his. "And I you."

When he kissed her this time, she could have sworn she heard someone laughing. Was it that man dancing on the last star in the handle of the Big Dipper? Or the angels rejoicing with them?

THE STORY BEHIND *THIS* STORY

D o you think you could do a Christmas novella to be published with another author's novella?" How I love to hear invitations like that. I agreed, we discussed possibilities and I suggested this be set in Soldahl, North Dakota like the others. The strange thing—some would call it a coincidence, but I call a God-cidence—was that a reader had just asked me what about the children of the characters she had grown to love. She wanted to know what happens to them. So did I.

I thanked her, tickled that she cared for my characters that much, because I sure did. But—a big one in my mind—I did not want to write about World War I or any war. I wrote The Secret Refuge series set during the Civil War, but that was more about saving a family's Thoroughbred horses from being killed during the battles. I really did not want get into another war.

"But you can write about the people left behind at home and what happened to them because of their beloved young men going off to fight the Huns." My friend looked at me and shrugged. "Makes sense to me."

Put that way, it made sense to me too. If I did not have to include even one battle scene... And so the thinking began. What characters to use? Who would be the young man going off to war and the young woman staying at home? What had been happening the last five to seven years in Soldahl? Who, what and why, always the why—the why caused by what had gone on the their lives. Why do people do the things they do? In my writing world, we call that the backstory, not to be confused with the story behind the story.

One morning I woke up with a dream still fresh in my mind. Mostly we don't remember our dreams, more the sensations or a lingering feeling. This one left me waking with a smile and definite pictures. I made myself lie in bed and replay the dream because I knew if I got up and got going, the dream would probably do the same.

So who was the lovely young woman with her honey colored hair swept back in a clasp? Wearing a simple white waist and a dark ankle length skirt and walking along picking wild flowers?

I ran the list of older children in the last book through my mind. Why, Mary Moen would be the right age, she'd been a neat kid, now she'd be a beautiful young woman. Next question is always, what does my character want? Of course. She who helped her mother raise the younger family members and loved school now dreams of teaching other people's children. She never tried to figure out how many times she and the younger children in their family and some others played school, with her always the teacher.

But who was that boy who was now a young man I saw in the dream? The red hair gave him away. Will Dunfey, of course. The blacksmith, Dag Weinlander's assistant.

I love it when I go to bed asking a question and the answer is there in the morning, not necessarily in a dream like this one had been, but more ideas parading through my mind. Either way, our unconscious mind never goes to sleep, so at night I give it something specific to do. What a gift God gave us in our unconscious or sub-conscious mind. And most of us don't intentionally use it much. I love Psalm 139 where it talks about us being fearfully and wonderfully made. We are indeed.

So we say goodbye to the characters of Soldahl,

North Dakota. And no, I do not plan to write more about them, but I know the stories continue because that is the way life is. Thank you for celebrating twenty-five years of stories with me. I hope reading my books reminds you of stories from your life, the laughing one and the crying ones. Remember always, sharing joys doubles them and sharing sorrows, cuts them in half.

Blessings always,

Lauraine

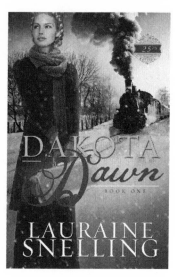

Dakota Dawn
Book One

"Soldahl! Next stop, Soldahl!"

When Nora Johanson hears the conductor's words, her heart begins to race. At least she will be in the arms of the man she has promised to marry—Hans Larson. At fifteen, she was so sure of their love. Now, three years later and far from the mountains and fjords of her beloved homeland, Norway, she wonders...

She steps off the train, finds her trunk full of hand-embroidered linens, quilts, and household treasures painted with rosemaling designs, and looks anxiously for Hans. The pelting March snow stings her cheeks.

"Where is he? Dear God, what will I do?"

When Hans fails to arrive at the train station that night, Nora finds herself thrown into a life she never expected with people she doesn't know—Reverend and Mrs. Moen and Carl Detschman, a grieving German immigrant. Is this really what God had planned for her?

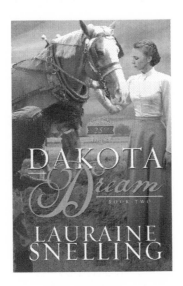

Dakota Dream
Book Two

"I CAME TO AMERICAN EXPECTING TO BE MARRIED."

Clara Johanson has a ticket to America and a photograph of a blond, curly-haired, blue-eyed man to prove her point. But when she arrives in Soldahl, North Dakota, the man who meets her at the train station, Dag Weinlander, is definitely not blond and, to make matters worse, he obviously hasn't bathed in days.

At least she knows she will see joy in her sister's face when she surprises her by arriving at her Soldahl home.

As Clara begins her unexpected life as a single, Norwegian immigrant, she experiences the truth of God's Word that "weeping may endure for a night, but joy cometh in the morning." Along the way she helps others, even Dag Weinlander, experience that truth too, as she steps into a new Dakota Dream far different than the one that brought her all the way from Bergen, Norway.

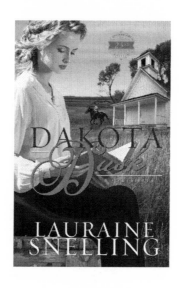

Dakota Dusk
Book Three

JUDE WEINLANDER HAS THE FACE OF AN ANGEL...BUT THE
HEART OF A BULLY AND A CHEAT.

"It ain't fair," Jude grumbled. "My brother, the dolt himself,
has a thriving business, a beautiful wife, and that grand house
of his. It just ain't fair, I tell ya."

When fire rages through his childhood home one night,
Jude, full of anger and guilt, turns his back on his family who
can help him heal. He leaves Soldahl, North Dakota, and takes
up wandering from town to town.

When he arrives in the small, fire-ravaged town of Willowford, North Dakota, he agrees to help schoolmarm Rebekka
Stenesrude by rebuilding the schoolhouse before he moves on,
once again.

But God keeps Jude in Willowford to work on his heart,
teaching him that for every dusk there is a sunrise.

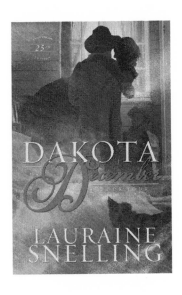

Dakota December
Book Four

"HELP." A WEAK VOICE MOANED FROM THE HORSE'S BACK.

Sheriff Caleb Stenesrude climbs over the gate in a blizzard and reaches up in time to catch the woman as she falls. To his astonishment, a small child, hanging on for dear life, falls with her.

Under his breath he thanks the good Lord for bringing them this far and for a dog with a nose and ears to beat all.

As the North Dakota storm continues to scream outside the house on the edge of town, Caleb tries to tend to the near-frozen mother and boy. When the woman lets out a piercing cry of labor, Caleb realizes this would be a Christmas eve like no other.

In the days after, Caleb and the town of Soldahl take Johanna Carlson and her two children into their hearts, but Johanna keeps her distance, afraid to tell anyone the truth about her life.